Running the Risk

Lesley Choyce

orca soundings

ORCA BOOK PUBLISHERS

For Aidan

Library and Archives Canada Cataloguing in Publication

Choyce, Lesley, 1951-
Running the risk / written by Lesley Choyce.

(Orca soundings)
ISBN 978-1-55469-026-8 (bound).--ISBN 978-1-55469-025-1 (pbk.)

I. Title. II. Series: Orca soundings

PS8555.H668 R84 2009 jC813'.54 C2009-900273-6

Summary: After being the victim of an armed robbery, Sean goes in search of more danger.

First published in the United States, 2009
Library of Congress Control Number: 2009920381

Orca Book Publishers gratefully acknowledges the support for its publishing programs provided by the following agencies: the Government of Canada through the Book Publishing Industry Development Program and the Canada Council for the Arts, and the Province of British Columbia through the BC Arts Council and the Book Publishing Tax Credit.

Cover design by Teresa Bubela
Cover photography by Getty Images

ORCA BOOK PUBLISHERS
PO Box 5626, STN. B
VICTORIA, BC CANADA
V8R 6S4

ORCA BOOK PUBLISHERS
PO Box 468
CUSTER, WA USA
98240-0468

www.orcabook.com
Printed and bound in Canada.
Printed on 100% PCW recycled paper.
12 11 10 09 • 4 3 2 1

Chapter One

The gunmen arrived at Burger Heaven shortly after midnight on Friday. I was on the frontline, taking orders along with Lacey and Cam. It was like a dream at first. The place had been quiet except for some workmen laughing over their French fries, and a couple of slightly drunk kids from school goofing around at a table by the windows.

And then the door opened and two guys with ski masks on walked in nervously. One walked straight to me. The other went to

Lacey. As they approached, the guns came up. Lacey, Cam and I froze. The room suddenly went dead quiet except for the sound of hamburgers sizzling in the back and the buzz of the overhead fluorescent lights. I'd never even noticed the hum of the fluorescent lights before.

The guy with the gun pointed at Lacey spoke first. "Open it, girl."

Lacey froze.

"I said open it."

The guy with the gun on me said nothing. I was looking at Lacey. And then at Cam. There was a panic button on the floor beneath each register. A silent alarm. You triggered it and the cops would know we were in trouble. I saw Cam looking down at the floor.

But something told me that right here, right now, hitting that button would be the wrong thing to do. These two guys were nervous. I was looking my gunman right in the eyes. I knew there was something there. These guys were whacked on something. Anything could make them freak. The guns were real. Everything was real.

And that's when it kicked in.

This feeling of calm.

"Be cool," I said to the guy pointing the gun at Lacey. Then I looked at the guy with the gun on me. I stared straight into his eyes, and then I looked at the barrel of the gun like it was no big deal.

"I'm going to push this key and the drawer will open," I said. "Okay?"

My gunman nodded. I pushed the key, and the drawer opened. I saw one of the workmen get up. At first I thought he was going to try to do something. And I didn't want that.

But I was wrong. First he and then his buddy got up and slipped out the front door. Lacey's gunman turned and aimed in their direction. He pulled the trigger and the shot was deafening. "Shit," was all he said. The bullet must have hit the ceiling because no glass shattered. He turned back quickly and pushed the gun into Lacey's face.

"Here," I said, cleaning all the bills out of my register and handing them across the counter. "Now I'll get you the rest," I said.

"Yeah," my gunman said.

I walked to Lacey and made sure it was obvious what I was doing. I hit the key, the drawer opened and I offered over more bills.

Then I walked over to Cam's station and did the same. It was only money. Nothing to die for, that's for sure. It was all clear as day in my head.

The two gunmen stuffed the money into their coat pockets, turned and ran. As soon as they were out the door and away from the parking lot, I hit the silent alarm.

Lacey began to cry and Cam said the stupidest thing in the world. "Why'd you give them the money?"

"You all right, Lacey?" I asked.

"No, Sean," she said, "I'm not all right."

"What were you thinking?" Cam asked. Somehow he wasn't getting it.

The kids at the table were standing up now. "I don't freaking believe it," one of them said and then puked on the floor.

Riley and Jeanette, who'd been listening

from the food-prep area, came up to the counter now.

"Is everyone all right?" Riley asked.

"Yeah, we're all alive anyway," I said.

"Did you see what this jerk did?" Cam said, pointing at me.

"Yeah," Jeanette said. "I saw what he did. He saved you from getting killed."

Cam looked mad. He looked at me like it was all my fault.

The kids at the table out front were helping their buddy who had just barfed on the floor get himself together. Then they headed for the door. I probably should have asked them to stay until the cops came, but I didn't. I understood they wanted to get the hell out of here. I knew who they were, so I didn't bother to ask them to stay. The police could find them for information if they needed to.

Jeanette was holding Lacey.

Cam was blathering. "This isn't worth it," he said. "I'm quitting this stupid job. Now." He walked around the counter and kicked over a chair. Then he left. I didn't ask him to stay either.

When the police arrived, two officers in bulletproof vests pushed open the glass door and walked in, guns raised. I watched their eyes as they looked at us and then scanned Burger Heaven. I noticed the buzz of the lights again.

"They're gone," I said.

The guns came down and the cops moved forward.

"Anyone hurt?" one of them asked. Two more policemen came in the door.

"No," I said. "I think we're okay."

"Do you know which way they went?"

I shook my head no.

One of the policemen saw the bullet hole in the ceiling. "You guys had a close call," he said. "That wasn't a cap gun."

It was about then that I noticed something about the way I was feeling. My heart was still pumping so loud I could hear it in my ears, and my breathing was a bit ragged.

But the weird part was that I was feeling great. And I'd been feeling this way from the moment the robber put the gun up to my face.

Chapter Two

We told the story to the police and I got a ride home in a police car and went to bed. I didn't bother to wake my parents. They would get the news from the paper in the morning.

I didn't sleep much. Adrenaline, I guess. I kept wondering why I had kept my cool. And why I had been absolutely certain there was only one thing to do. I knew that if Cam had tried to hit that alarm while the robbers were there, somebody would have been killed. At the time I was operating on pure instinct—and adrenaline, of course.

Afterward, lying in bed, the rational part of my brain was thinking, *Yeah, those guys could have fired their guns at any moment.* Anything could have happened.

I was fuzzy-headed in the morning and tired. All the adrenaline had worn off, I suppose.

My father woke me up. He was dressed for work at the casino. The newspaper was in his hand. "Why didn't you wake us?"

"Nobody got hurt. It turned out fine."

My mother was in my bedroom now too. "Sean, you could have..." She couldn't finish the sentence.

"I could have but I wasn't," I said. "What time is it?"

My parents looked puzzled. "I think you need to stay home today," my father said. "You need to rest."

"I don't feel like resting."

"We tried to tell you that job could be dangerous," my mother said.

"It wasn't like I was looking for trouble."

But I had asked for the late shift, for both Friday and Saturday night. I could have worked during the day on Sunday or even from four to ten in the evening. But I had convinced my parents everything would be okay. And I loved the fact that all kinds of weird crap happened late at night. I even liked the walk home on the dark streets. Had I been secretly hoping for something like this to happen?

"Well, you're not going back there to work," my father said.

"I don't want to quit."

"We'll find you another job."

"Yeah, right. Like at the casino, I suppose." This was a sore spot. My father had lost his job with the insurance company and had taken on an administration job at the casino. He'd always told me he didn't approve of gambling, and then he hired on to a place that was solely dependent on taking suckers' money when the odds were stacked way too high against them.

"You know you're too young. They can't hire you."

"Be reasonable," my mother said. "Besides, you don't need to work."

"I need to do something," I said. Because of last night, because of the way I felt, I'd had my first taste of some other world. It was almost like I'd been sleeping most of my life. Whatever I'd felt last night, I wanted to feel again.

"I'll fix you some breakfast," my mother said.

"And then I'll take you down to the police station," my father said. "They called. They want to ask some more questions."

"Don't you have to work today?" I asked. "You always work on Saturday."

"After I read the paper, I decided to take the day off."

My father drove me to the police station. We passed by Burger Heaven. It was closed, with yellow police tape around it. There were a few police cars in the lot, and I figured an investigation of some sort was underway.

I sat in a room with a man who introduced himself as Detective Solway. He insisted my father wait outside.

Solway said, "The officer on the scene said you were remarkably calm about the whole thing."

"Not really," I said. "It scared the crap out of me."

"But the other workers said you kept your cool. One even said that you acted like you knew this was going to happen."

"That idiot, Cam. If he had moved to push the silent alarm, he would have been dead."

"How do you know that?"

"Those guys were antsy."

"So you just opened all three drawers and gave them what they wanted."

"Yes."

"Why?"

"Because it was the rational thing to do."

Detective Solway just stared at me.

"Do you think I actually had something to do with the robbery?" I was surprised, of course. But in an odd way I was almost flattered. No one had ever accused me of anything seriously bad. Because I'd never really done anything seriously bad. Because I didn't take chances.

Solway shook his head. "No. I don't think so. We already did a background check. Your high school principal said you must be a good kid because he had never even heard of you, couldn't put a face to the name."

"It's a big high school."

"Yeah, but troublemakers stand out. And you didn't. B average, the records say. Not bad."

"More like B minus these days. I've been slipping."

"Could be the late-night job."

"What are the odds of a scene like last night happening again? At Burger Heaven, I mean."

"Not that great. Once a place gets hit, we keep a closer eye on it, and the bad guys know that."

"Any leads?"

"A couple. Could you identify either of the men if you saw them?"

"I doubt it."

"A lot of people are pretty shaken up after an event like that."

"Traumatized?"

"Yeah, traumatized. But you seem to be rather cocky about it all."

I figured that Solway detected that something was different about me. Being questioned like this had almost brought the adrenaline buzz back. And I liked that. I was a different person from the one who had gone to work last night. And even the principal of my school—my huge high school—now knew who I was.

"We're done," Solway said.

"That's it?"

"Well, keep in mind you were lucky. You could have been killed."

"I know that," I said.

"Then why are you smiling?"

I didn't answer him. I hadn't realized it, but I had been smiling all through the interview. And I didn't know why.

Chapter Three

I have always been pretty ordinary. No one expected too much of me. I was an only child, and my parents were pretty overprotective. When I rode a bike, I wore a helmet. When I skateboarded—not for long—I had the helmet, plus the pads for knees and elbows. My parents pretty much drove me anywhere I needed to go.

School was easy and I didn't have to try that hard. I'd had a couple of girlfriends but they were more like friends than girlfriends.

At sixteen I was a virgin, and it was not a big deal to me. Sure, I was horny sometimes, but actually having sex with a girl seemed so... well, complicated, that I wondered if it was worth it. And there were STDs to worry about and possible pregnancy and even AIDS.

Are you starting to get the picture?

The job at Burger Heaven was an out-there thing for me. My father tried to convince me not to take it and said he'd up my allowance. My mother said I should concentrate on school and my "social life."

"What social life?" I had countered.

And then I was in line at Burger Heaven one day and saw the sign for help wanted. The kids who worked there seemed to be kind of a team. They acted as if they liked each other, and I could see they helped each other out. I mean, I know what people think about working at burger joints. Not too glamorous, for sure. Crummy pay. Not a heck of a lot of excitement. Stupid uniforms. Free greasy food that would give you pimples.

But I asked for a form, filled it out and got a job. Hey, they were desperate. They would have hired anyone with arms and legs. And like I said, I could have worked an easier shift. But I wanted the night thing. I was just tired of taking the easy route, the safe route, with everything. I wanted the night shift.

And got it. My parents were not happy.

It was exciting in a way. Staying up late. Weirdos coming in stoned or drunk. Hookers showed up sometimes. And creepy people who looked like they were dangerous. Sometimes the customers were rude. Sometimes they were funny. Sometimes downright friendly. Aside from the students who came in, most of these customers were unlike anyone I knew. These were the people my parents had been protecting me from all my life.

The day after the robbery, my boss, Ernesto, called to say I shouldn't come back to work for a week. "You're on what we call stress leave," he said over the phone. "It's a company policy."

"Like if you work for the airline and survive a plane crash?" I asked.

"Something like that. It's a mental-health thing."

"But I don't feel stressed. I could come back to work tonight."

"No. Don't worry. You'll get paid anyway."

But I wasn't worrying about the pay. I wanted to be back at work.

"We're going to stay closed for a couple of days anyway and then reopen. Cam quit and so did Lacey. If you feel like doing the same, I'd understand."

"No. It's okay, really. I'll be back in a week."

"Suit yourself. And, hey, thanks for being cool through the whole thing. Seems like you kept your head."

"Yeah."

I hung up and relived the whole experience one more time. And then suddenly I felt the walls closing in around me. I started to feel really antsy. I had to get out of there.

My cell phone rang as I was leaving the house.

"Sean? It's me, Jeanette." She had never called me before.

"Did Ernesto call you?" she asked.

"Yep. You on stress leave too?" I said.

"Yes. And I can use it. I'm not sure I want to go back after that. Do you?"

"Yeah, I do. Isn't that funny?"

"A little. But then, you acted different from the rest of us."

"I did what I had to do," I said.

I couldn't exactly figure out why she was calling me or even how she got my cell phone number. But I pictured her in my mind. Long dark hair, usually under one of those stupid net caps at work, and kind of sexy.

"Want to go get a coffee?" I asked. "I'm just leaving my house and heading out."

"Sure," she said. "Meet you at Tim Hortons on Queen Street. In thirty minutes."

"See you there," I said as I closed the phone. I was surprised that I had been so forward.

Chapter Four

On the way to Tim Hortons, I did something strange. I closed my eyes and kept them closed as I walked.

I used to do this when I was a kid—in an open field, with no one around, with nothing to bump into. And I'd count the seconds. When I got to thirty, something would make me open my eyes. I knew I wasn't going to bump into anything. I knew I wasn't going to fall off a cliff. At worst I'd trip and fall down on the grass. But I couldn't get past thirty. Thirty seconds with my eyes closed seemed like a long time. Some primitive part of my brain always forced my eyes open.

The sidewalk was straight. I knew the suburban neighborhood I was walking through. There were a few people around, but I figured they'd get out of my way. And I counted to thirty. The impulse to open my eyes was strong, but I fought it. I squeezed my eyelids shut tighter. I heard some people walking past me, and they were laughing. Even that didn't make me open my eyes.

But the tree did. The tree had decided it wasn't going to get out of my way. It was staying put. I'd made it to forty-two seconds. A record.

If anyone had been watching, they must have thought I was beyond stupid.Needless to say, I kept my eyes open the rest of the way downtown.

Jeanette was already in the coffee shop. She waved as I walked in.

"What happened to your nose?" she asked.

"Disagreement with another life form," I said, touching the tip of my nose and discovering it had been scratched. "Hey, thanks for coming," I said. I wanted to change the subject.

"I'm surprised you asked."

"Me too."

"We've been working together for months. How come you ask me out for coffee today?"

"I don't know. Why did you say yes?"

"I don't know. I guess I realized you were more interesting than I thought."

"Can I take that as a compliment?"

"Sure." Jeanette smiled at me, and then she took something out of her pocket. She set a perfectly rolled, rather fat joint down on the table between us. "We're on stress leave, right?" she said.

I didn't know what to say.

"C'mon," she said, taking a gulp of her coffee and retrieving the joint.

I followed her outside, and we walked behind the coffee shop. We didn't go far. She sat down on the curb in the back and, in full view of the cars lined up for the drive-through, lit the joint with a lighter. Jeanette inhaled deeply and then passed it to me. At first I thought it was a joke. I mean, here we were, toking up, with people looking right at us. But I decided what the hell.

I sucked in the smoke and, of course, coughed. I'd only smoked a couple of times before and never particularly liked it that much, but I couldn't turn down a beautiful girl passing me some weed. I handed the joint back to her and found myself smiling at the scowling woman in the Toyota who was looking straight at me.

The second time I didn't cough. I was more cautious. This stuff was clearly stronger than anything I'd experienced. Jeanette had taken on a kind of dreamy look, and I found myself drifting up into the sky.

When I brought my gaze back down to earth, I realized that the rear door of the coffee shop had opened, and someone who might've been the manager of the place was headed our way. Time to leave the premises.

We both got up and started walking away.

"Why did we just do that?" I asked.

"Do what?"

"Sit there in public and smoke a joint."

"It was a kind of test," she said.

"Of me?"

"Of both of us."

"You don't normally do that sort of thing?" I asked.

"No. But it seemed all right since you were with me."

"Do you get high a lot?"

"Not usually. Today seemed different."

"Then I must be a bad influence on you," I said.

"Hey, lighten up," she said.

And then she kissed me hard on the mouth.

Chapter Five

We sat on a bench in the park and made out for a while. Jeanette was very stoned and very sexy. I began to consider what I'd been missing. It occurred to me that the girl was trouble but I didn't care. Maybe trouble was what I needed to make my life a little more interesting.

And then suddenly she pulled back from me and checked her watch. "Damn. Gotta go," she said. "Big Sunday dinner with my folks. And I'm starving." She kissed me one more time on the lips and then left.

I sat there for a few minutes, suddenly not feeling all that good. I touched the scratch on my nose and remembered the tree. Then I found myself looking up into the branches of the trees around me, and I watched the patterns of the sunlight coming through the leaves.

Trees reminded me of my grandfather, my father's father, who had died when I was twelve. The trees had killed him.

Well, maybe it wasn't the trees' fault, but at the moment it seemed that way. I missed him, even now.

He had insisted I not call him Granddad or Grandpop or anything like that. His name was Henry and he liked to be called Hank. "Like Hank Williams or Hank Snow or Hank Aaron," he'd say, although none of those names meant much to me.

My father was always busy and never did a lot of father-son things with me. He worked for an insurance company for a long time, and he'd work weekends if he had to. Right up to the time he was fired and had to look for a new career. Hank wasn't like that. Hank would show up on a Saturday with the top down on his Mustang convertible. He'd drive me anywhere I wanted to go. During my skateboarding phase, he would even take me to the skateboard park and join me. The kids all laughed at him when he fell, but he didn't care.

Can you picture some kid's grandfather on a half-pipe? That was Hank. "Sean, you only get to live once," he'd say. "And you can't just sit on your ass and watch the world go by."

He made a living by building homemade ultralight aircraft. He'd make one at a time and then sell it. I don't think he made a ton of money but he liked what he did. I was never allowed to fly with him in his noisy, two-person, totally-open-cockpit planes. Not even once. He and my father argued about that a hundred times. And my mother told Hank that if he didn't stop asking about it, he wouldn't be allowed to hang out with me at all.

And so I think Hank must have really liked me as a grandson because he stopped asking. Instead of flying, we hiked. And sometimes we swam in a deep abandoned quarry where every sound echoed off the cliff walls. And it was there, with the safety of deep water beneath us, that he tried to teach me to rock climb—barefooted in a bathing suit, using nothing but fingers and feet to climb a sheer rock wall.

I never got very high. I fell a few times and it felt like I was going to die. Hank would climb way up to a ledge and then do a cannonball into the water. He'd surface with a big grin on his face. My parents never found out about the quarry or the rock climbing. They just thought we were swimming in the public pool. It was a secret I kept even after Hank was gone. And it was a secret Hank took to his grave.

The first ultralight crash didn't kill him. The engine conked out, and he said he was pretty sure he could glide in to safety but the wind suddenly switched. "And the ground came up and grabbed me," he said, always enjoying the reports of his own near-death disasters.

The second crash involved a neighbor's shed. "The man just can't die," he'd said, having walked away from that one with no more damage than an angry neighbor and a lot of work repairing the ultralight.

It was the third crash that did him in. Turned out the immortal Hank could die after all, although it must have come as quite a shock to his system. People who watched him crash said that if he had just been able to keep his machine up for another fifty feet, he would have been past the trees. But it was the trees that got him. Big tall ones—white pine and maple and spruce. They had his number.

I sat there alone on the bench, the taste of Jeanette still in my mouth, and I wondered where the spirit of my grandfather was just then. And I realized how much I still missed him.

On my way home, I had to cross a four-lane highway. There was a lot of Sunday-afternoon traffic and there was no place for a pedestrian to cross. In fact, I stood by the side of the road waiting for a break, thinking maybe someone would see me and cars would let me cross.

But it wasn't like that. Everyone was on their way somewhere. And in a damn hurry.

I don't know why, but that made me angry.

So I focused on the far side of the road—where I wanted to be—and I just started walking. Straight across. I didn't even look to the side. I just kept walking.

I heard the car horns and I heard some tires screeching and I still didn't look. And then I heard some angry voices. A man and a couple of women yelling something at me.

But no one actually stopped.

I arrived at the other side of the road, and after those honking, cursing drivers had passed, it was as if nothing had happened. The stream of traffic just kept going. I stopped being angry and I laughed out loud.

Chapter Six

When I read the report in the newspaper about the robbery, it seemed like something completely different from what I had experienced. No one's name was reported except for the owner's, Ernesto Millard. He was quoted as saying, "No one was hurt, and we assume that there was really no gun, just someone with something that looked like a gun."

Well, Ernesto Millard was not even there. And yes, it was a gun. Not something that "looked like a gun." There was even a bullet hole in the ceiling if anyone wanted to see proof. But Ernesto wanted to make people feel safe about going back to Burger Heaven. He knew something like this might hurt business. He had even phoned my house and talked to my father, suggesting that my dad urge me not to talk too much about what happened.

At school on Monday, I looked at the faces of my classmates. I noticed some of them looking at me kind of funny. At first I thought maybe it was all in my head, but then I saw Cam hanging out with a couple of his friends, Nick and Deacon. I could imagine Cam had told them his version of the events.

I ran into Deacon later that day in the washroom. We were standing beside each other at the urinals. "You must have been scared pretty bad to just hand over all the cash," he said. He was smiling as he said it.

So that had been Cam's story—his version of what happened. I was trying to come up with something to say to set the record straight. I understood immediately that if

Deacon thought that's what happened, pretty soon that would be what most of the kids in school would think. But I figured that whatever I said to him right there wouldn't make much difference. So I turned slightly and pissed on Deacon's shoes. Maybe I got a little on his pant leg.

"Oh, sorry, man," I said. "Guess I have bad aim."

Deacon was shell-shocked. He said nothing. I zipped up and left.

It took me a little time to get settled after that. If anyone asked Lacey or Jeanette, they would get the real story, but as I headed to English class, I was beginning to realize something. The newspaper story. Cam's version. The official police version of the event. There were so many different ways to view things. What did it matter what people believed had happened? To hell with what anyone wanted to think about me.

I had a quick flash of an image of the gun aimed right at me, of the eyes of the young guy holding the gun. The intense crazy eyes of someone who could lose it at any second.

And then it was gone.

I walked into Mrs. Ryerson's classroom and noticed the kids looking at me again. I wanted to yell at them. But I didn't. I slid into a seat and opened my book.

"How many of you liked Shirley Jackson's story, 'The Lottery'?" Mrs. Ryerson asked.

It had been the weekend reading assignment. I'd read the story Friday right after school, right before going to work. It was a weird story, for sure. Something about a town and a lottery where the "winner" gets stoned to death by the townspeople. I couldn't say I liked it, but it was interesting.

Julie Coles raised her hand. "I thought it was great. I mean, it wasn't a happy story but it had a lot of meaning." Her answers were almost always vague and elusive. She thought she'd get a better grade in school if she answered questions in class, even if she didn't really have anything to say.

The door opened and Deacon walked in.

Mrs. Ryerson looked at him but didn't say anything. She'd make a note that he was late for class. That was her way of doing things. Three notes for being late and you'd be in trouble. I looked at Deacon's shoes. They were still wet. I smiled.

"Yes," Mrs. Ryerson said, "the story did have a lot of meaning. It could mean many things. It was an allegory, perhaps. What kinds of lotteries do we participate in?"

"Scratch and Win," someone said. "And the Six Forty-Nine. You pay some money and you have a chance at winning a lot of money."

"True," the teacher said, "but if you win Shirley Jackson's lottery, you don't get something good, you get something bad."

I found myself taking a deep breath. I felt the need to talk. "It's all a lottery," I said. "Like if you're lucky, you get born here and have lots of everything you need. If you're not lucky, you're born in a third world country and starve or get sick and die."

"That's interesting, Sean," Mrs. Ryerson said. I knew she was probably shocked. I hadn't opened my mouth once in class since the beginning of the year. "But what about the element of violence in the story?" she asked. "What about the way it ends?"

She was looking straight at me now and so were the other students. I don't think she knew that I'd been working at Burger Heaven the night of the robbery. They knew—my classmates—or at least they thought they knew what happened. But she didn't. So, in my own head, the set-up was pretty interesting. And I had read the story. It had made me think.

"The townspeople throw rocks and kill their neighbor. Then they go back to their normal, happy daily lives."

"Yes. It's disturbing, isn't it?"

"Disturbing, right. But maybe that's the way it really is. Maybe we're throwing stones at the victims every day in order to protect our comfortable, safe lives. The homeless, the poor, the crazy ones. I think it's just the luck of the draw that we're not one of them, and if we were, we'd see everything differently."

"Interesting," Mrs. Ryerson said again and then moved on.

Which was a good thing, since I wasn't sure where I was going with this. It was only a story, right? We were just doing that English-class thing of "discussing" it, trying to find out what it meant.

"I don't think the story meant that at all," Julie said, and she prattled on with something that didn't make much sense to me or anyone else, but I was glad the spotlight was off me.

I settled back into my seat and looked around at my classmates. Each of them had won or lost several important lotteries. Brains. Looks. Parents. Health. And I suddenly realized I didn't truly know anything about any of their lives.

I looked out the window at a crow sitting on the branch of a dead tree. The crow seemed to know immediately that I was looking at him, and he didn't like it. He looked right at me and then spread his wings and flew. And as I watched his black image move on up into the sky, I thought about my grandfather again. And I missed him so badly I thought I would cry.

Chapter Seven

I was headed to the cafeteria when Jeanette found me. She had a frantic look in her eyes and I wondered if she'd been toking again.

"Sean, I've been looking all over for you." She grabbed my arm and squeezed so tightly that it hurt.

"Hey, easy," I said. "What's up?"

"I'm having a panic attack."

"A what?"

"Anxiety. I'm, like, freaking out. It's happened before. I have to get out of here. Will you go with me?"

"Go where?"

"Anywhere."

"Now?"

She seemed to be having a hard time breathing. "Yes. I have to get out of here now."

"Sure," I said, not knowing what I was getting myself into. "Let's go."

We left school and started walking quickly. She began to calm down, and we slowed our pace. "What was that all about?" I asked.

"Something happens in my head. I can't quite explain it. I was just sitting in math class, hoping I wouldn't be called on. I started to get kind of nervous—stressed-out. And then panicky. I had to leave class. Mr. Boyd asked me to sit back down and that made it worse. So I left the room. And came looking for you."

"Why me?"

"I feel safe around you."

I guess I felt flattered just then. I put my arm around her, and she tucked into my side as we walked.

I thought that the "right" thing to do would be to go to the office and maybe see if one of the counselors could talk to her. But I knew she didn't want that. And neither did I. I liked the way this made me feel. I felt important.

This was the first time I had ever walked out of school in the middle of the day. And it felt good. After a while I said, "Let's go downtown. Wanna catch the bus or just walk?"

"Let's just walk. It helps sometimes." Jeanette seemed a little calmer.

"What brings it on?" I asked.

"Could be almost anything. It's mostly in my head. I feel like everything is going out of control. I feel like I can't stand it anymore."

"Can't you just calm yourself down?"

"Sometimes. But not all the time. You ever feel this way?"

I thought about it. "I've felt depressed and felt like saying 'screw the world, to hell with it all.'"

"No. It's not like that. There's, like, a fire alarm going off in my head."

"That's the panic part?"

"Yeah. I want to scream."

"Do you want to scream now?"

"It's not as bad as before but, yes, I want to scream."

"Then let's scream. Together, okay? One, two, three..."

And then we both opened our mouths and screamed in tandem. Not a word, just a syllable. We were both looking up at the sky as we did it. And then we looked at each other. And laughed.

I noticed a man walking his dog across the street. Both he and his dog had stopped in their tracks and looked over at us. The man's face said it all—we were a pair of dangerous teenagers up to no good. Then the dog started barking at us.

I made eye contact with the man and he scowled. I looked back at Jeanette. "Don't worry about him. Let's go." And we walked on.

"Wanna smoke some weed?" she asked. "That helps calm me down sometimes."

"No," I said, "but you can if you want to." It was funny. I liked the way I was feeling just then and didn't want to alter it in any way.

"I'll save it then. Sometimes I need it to get to sleep at night."

"Brain won't shut off?"

"Something like that."

We were headed away from the manicured lawns now, away from the suburban homes and into the older part of town. This was the south end of Main Street, with empty storefronts, some of the older mom-and-pop stores and a few small dingy-looking restaurants. It had been a while since I'd even walked down here and I wondered why I'd chosen to come this way.

"Where are we going?" Jeanette asked.

"Don't know," I said. "I guess I just wasn't in the mood for hanging out at the mall and getting harassed by the security goons. I kind of prefer the ambience here."

"Ambience?"

"It was on the vocabulary list in Mrs. Ryerson's class a while ago. It means atmosphere, how the environment of a place makes you feel."

And it was right about then that someone came up from behind and walloped me on the head with something that knocked me to my knees.

Chapter Eight

Jeanette screamed again, but this time it sounded different. I had been hit from behind. As I turned and got to my feet, I realized I had not been hurt. Whatever had conked me in the head had not been all that deadly.

I saw an older woman in a dirty ski jacket. She was glaring at me and holding her assault weapon, a gym bag of some sort. "There you are, Doyle. There you are. I've been looking all over for you and you've had me worried sick."

Her eyes were angry and her face was contorted. She was big and her hair was wild and messy.

"Leave us alone," Jeanette shouted at her.

The woman stared at Jeanette and then suddenly seemed confused. She looked back at me and then turned to go.

I noticed she was wearing running shoes that did not match. She was wearing men's pants as well. It was starting to sink in. I didn't know who she was. And I didn't know who Doyle was. I didn't really even care that she had just brought me to the ground, blindsided by a gym bag.

"Wait," I said.

At first she just walked on.

"Wait," I said again. "Please."

Jeanette gave me a wide-eyed look.

"It's okay," I said.

The woman turned and walked back toward us, her face softened now by something short of a smile. "I'm sorry, Doyle," she said. "It's just that I've been so worried about you." She hugged me then and began to cry.

She smelled bad. I wanted to push her away. I looked at Jeanette and could tell she was repulsed by the woman.

"Where have you been?" the woman asked me, pulling back a little and adjusting her ski jacket.

"School," I answered, for no clear reason. "I was in school."

"Oh," she said. "Of course. I guess I knew that. It's just that I was so worried." And then she turned to Jeanette. "Who's this?" she said suspiciously.

"Jeanette," I said. "She's my friend." I could tell that Jeanette wanted us to turn around and get the hell out of there.

A couple of old men walked by, sharing a bottle of something. They watched us but didn't say anything. One nodded at the woman though and said, "Lovely day, Priscilla, ain't it?" But she didn't say anything back.

"Your name's Priscilla?" I asked her.

"Of course. But don't you start addressing your mother by her first name."

"I'm not...," I began but cut myself off.

"You've grown so big," she said.

"Do you need some money or something?" I asked.

"No, Doyle. Of course not. Everything is fine." She did a little tidying act, almost as if she were looking at herself in the mirror. "What about you, do you need any money? Have you spent your allowance?"

Jeanette was tilting her head, giving me that let's-get-the-heck-out-of-here look. But I couldn't seem to make myself just walk away.

"No," I said. "I've still got some left. Are you hungry?" I pointed toward the Chinese restaurant nearby.

"Well, yes. But we can't go in there."

"Why not?"

"I'm not allowed in there."

I wasn't sure I needed to hear the story. "Then I'll go in that store over there and get us something."

"Okay," she said. "I would love a cheese sandwich and a bag of chips."

"Sure," I said.

Jeanette walked with me into the store. I looked over my shoulder and saw Priscilla sit down on her gym bag right there on the sidewalk.

"Let's just head back to school," Jeanette said. "I'm better now."

"Not yet," I said. "She thinks I'm her son. I can't just leave her there."

"Sean, are you crazy? You don't know anything about her. She could be dangerous."

Somehow that word confirmed the fact I would go back to Priscilla. Not that I wanted her to be dangerous. I just knew I had to go back to her. All she wanted was a cheese sandwich and a bag of potato chips.

And a son. She desperately needed a son.

"Okay. I'm going to go back to school by myself. I don't like it here. Besides, I've got a test in chemistry this afternoon. If I miss it, I'm going to flunk the course."

I was torn. I didn't like the idea of Jeanette walking back alone. "I'll walk you as far as the police station." That was only three blocks away.

"No thanks," she said coldly. And she left.

I paid for the sandwich and chips and went back outside. I watched Jeanette walking away and then I went to sit with Priscilla. I gave her the chips and the sandwich. She opened the sandwich and gave one half back to me.

"No thanks," I said. "I ate."

"Not junk food I hope," she said, biting into the sandwich and then opening up the chips.

"Not junk food," I said.

"That's good. You've always been a good boy, Doyle."

"Sean," I countered. "My name is Sean."

"Of course it is. You can choose any nickname you want."

I saw a tall young black man in a hoodie coming our way. He stopped right in front of us. "What's with you?" he asked me.

"She seemed hungry. I bought her some food."

"And?" His voice was hostile. "What are you doing here?"

I stood up. I felt a tingle of adrenaline. This time it wasn't a good feeling. "She thinks

I'm her son," I half whispered to him. We were looking at each other eye-to-eye now. He didn't blink. I was trying to remember something we studied in school about what it meant when someone didn't blink.

"Man," he said. "This woman thinks *I'm* her son some days."

"Doyle, right?"

He blinked and let out a little snort, something not quite a laugh. "Yeah, Doyle," he said. And then he cupped his hand over his mouth and leaned a little toward me. "But Doyle's been dead for a long time. Long time."

Chapter Nine

Priscilla seemed happy eating the sandwich and the chips. I gave her a smile. The black guy was reaching into his pocket for something. He was still looking at me in a hard way, sizing me up—my clothes, my hair. He was doing inventory.

"So?" I said, looking him in the eye.

"What do you mean?"

"So what's your, um, your analysis of me?"

"Analysis?" His eyes never left mine. Some kind of test. I noticed the hand was coming out of the pocket. "Gum?"

"What?"

"You want a piece of gum?" He was holding a pack of gum out to me.

"Sure." I popped one from the pack and handed it back. Priscilla saw the gum and bobbed her head.

"Sure thing, Priscilla," he said to her. "I bought it for you. Just finish your lunch first." Then he turned back to me. "They put way too much sugar and too many chemicals into chewing gum," the guy said.

"I bet they do," I said.

"So what is it, Save Seniors Day at the high school or something? You on a do-gooder field trip?"

I laughed. I could tell what he saw in me now. The analysis was complete.

"Something like that," I said.

"Monroe," he said. "My name's Monroe."

"I'm Sean. Does Priscilla live on the street?"

"Sometimes. Not all the time. She has a place she can stay at the women's shelter down the street. But she likes to wander."

"Isn't it dangerous?"

"Well, the alternative is they send her to an institution where they use restraints to keep her there."

"That would suck."

He nodded. "She'd die there and that would solve the problem of Priscilla."

I didn't exactly like the way he put that. Especially with her sitting so close.

"What I mean is it would solve the problem as far as the city was concerned."

"Do people on the street here give her a hard time?"

"Some do. And then some of us try to look out for her. Some of us she calls Doyle, some of us she calls by other rude names."

"But she likes you?"

"I buy her gum and play straight into the corporate agenda that is ruining our health." Monroe was smiling now. Guess I'd passed some kind of test. He popped a couple of pieces of gum out of the wrapper and handed them to Priscilla. She scooped them up and dropped them into her mouth.

That's when I noticed some other young guys coming our way. Four of them, looking like they just walked out of a rap video. Two of them were black and two of them were white. They stopped, and one of them poked Monroe on the arm. "Hanging out with old ladies again, Monroe," the guy said, looking at Priscilla and then at me. "We should introduce you to some younger women." He had obviously worked on his badass attitude.

"We all have our own versions of working the streets," Monroe said. "What's the word with you boys?"

I let them size me up. Seemed like a lot of analysis was going on in this neighborhood.

"Not much," was the answer.

I decided to play it low-key. I turned and smiled at Priscilla. Clearly she didn't see the four street kids as much of a threat. Then I looked at Monroe's friends—if they were friends. They were tough-looking, for sure. Dressed for the job. All attitude and bad posture. Not much older than me. I gave them a cool once-over and could feel the bad vibe but chose not to let it bother me.

"Sean," Monroe said, "this is Keeg, Vicente, Robert and J.L." Keeg was the one who'd poked Monroe. The other black guy was Vicente. They both met my eye. That wasn't the case for Robert and J.L., who just looked away as if I didn't matter.

I nodded at them but then spoke to Monroe. "Should I walk her back to the shelter?"

"Not a bad idea," Monroe said. He pointed up the street. "Three blocks that way and one block over on Prince Street. But she'll go only if she's ready to go." Then he turned to Priscilla.

"Priscilla, would you like this gentleman to walk you back home?"

She was looking up at the sky now. "It looks like it might rain," she said. The sun was shining brightly and there wasn't a cloud in the sky.

"Would you like me to walk you home?" I repeated the question.

She offered me her arm. "That would be lovely," she said.

Monroe smiled and looked down at the sidewalk. Keeg decided to spit on that same parcel of concrete. The others just stood there smirking.

"Good-bye, Doyle," she said to Monroe. "Be careful and have fun with your friends."

We turned and began to walk slowly toward the shelter. "I think I should take a nap when we get there," she said. "Do you think that is a good idea, Doyle?" Now I was back to being Doyle.

"I think that's a great idea. Did you like the sandwich?"

"I don't remember," she said, puzzled. "Do you think it will rain?"

"It might," I said as I guided her across the street. The light was green, but it went to yellow and then red, our crossing was so slow. Some idiot in an old Honda honked the horn at us, and I flashed the driver a dirty look. As soon as we were out of his way, he gunned the engine, shouted "Get off the street, Grandma!" and then sped away, leaving a trail of foul exhaust.

Chapter Ten

It was a slow hike to the women's shelter, and we had to stop several times along the way for Priscilla to rest and get her bearings. Sometimes she'd suddenly look at me with fear in her eyes and I'd try to calm her down. The only thing that worked was repeating "It's okay. It's me, Doyle. I'm walking you home."

People walking by would stare at her, and some would stare at both of us. They probably thought we were both crazy, homeless and wandering the streets instead of being confined to an institution where they thought we should be.

For the first time, I thought I knew what it felt like to be a street person. And it made me angry. But I didn't show that anger to Priscilla. The only thing that worked with Priscilla was gentleness. And I was more than a little surprised that I had that in me.

The Highfield Women's Shelter was an ugly three-story brick building on Prince Street. There was no sign out front. The door was locked. I rang the bell.

A large well-dressed woman answered the door. She had big muscular arms and looked like she lifted weights and was into bodybuilding. She smiled at Priscilla but glowered at me.

"Welcome back, Priscilla. How was your walkabout?"

"I'm rather tired, dear. And I think it's about to rain." She took a step inside and I started to follow her.

The woman stopped me. "Sorry, you can't come in here," she said to me rudely.

"I'd just like to get her settled in."

"You're not allowed. No men are allowed in here. It's the rule." I could tell by the tone of her voice that she either created the rule or totally approved of it.

"But I'm just trying to..."

"I know, you're just trying to help. Well, that's great. Thanks for bringing Priscilla back. She'll be fine."

Priscilla had let go of my arm and was inside now. She seemed calm enough. "Goodbye, Doyle," she said.

"Bye."

The woman stood there glaring at me, waiting for me to turn and leave. Why such hostility? I wondered.

"Is she going to be all right?" I asked.

"As well as can be expected."

"But is she going to wander off again?"

"Yes. We can't stop her."

"Can't or don't want to?" I asked, feeling a little defensive now.

"We do the best we can. She has no one. This is her life. You can't put people in cages." And with that the door closed in my face.

I met up with Jeanette as school was letting out. She seemed much calmer now but didn't seem all that thrilled to see me.

"Feeling better?" I asked.

"Yes, I took a couple of pills—Ativan. For the anxiety. Don't worry, they were prescribed. It makes school seem so much more enjoyable." There was an edge to her voice.

"I'm sorry about this morning."

"You shouldn't have made me walk back alone. You're not the person I thought you were. I guess I was wrong."

"I thought I should try to help that woman."

"I had another panic attack on the way back to school. That's why I had to take the Ativan. It was all your fault."

"Sorry."

"Do you have anything to drink at your house?" she asked.

"You mean like booze?"

"Of course. Something with alcohol."

"Maybe. My mother keeps a few bottles of wine around. Why? You want to come over to my house?"

"Yes."

"I thought you were angry at me."

"I am," she said and then stopped in her tracks. She walked closer to me and stood on her tiptoes and kissed me hard on the mouth. It made me dizzy. "So there."

But it was a weird kiss. As she was kissing me, she ground her teeth against mine. There was something forced about it. Something not quite right. But I liked it anyway.

My mother had a collection of about twelve wine bottles, I discovered. More than I had thought. There were four bottles of the same red French wine. I opened one of them, hoping she might not notice. Jeanette wanted to drink from the bottle, but I found a couple of glasses. And we headed to the rec room in the basement. If red wine was going to be spilled, I figured it would be safer down there than on our beige living-room carpet.

And sure enough, there was spillage. Jeanette's pills mixed with a little wine were probably a bad combination. I cut her off after two glasses.

"You're so protective," she said, her voice a little slurred. "I like that part. But you're also so, hmm, well, so *responsible*. What's with that?"

"It's the way I am, I guess." I took only small sips of the wine. It made my tongue feel funny. I wasn't much of a wine drinker.

"My parents would like you," she said with more than a little sarcasm in her voice.

"And that's bad, right?"

"That's very bad. Would your parents like me?"

With the top button of her blouse now unbuttoned and the drunk look on her face, the answer to that question was an easy one. But I didn't answer it.

"Well," she said, taking the last sip from her glass, "what do we do now?"

I didn't know what to do. I realized that here was a very attractive girl I could take advantage of, but the other part of my brain was screaming that I wanted her out of my house and safely in her own home.

"Now we go for a walk," I said. "I'll walk you all the way home. It'll help clear your head."

"What's with all the walking?" she asked.

"Only form of transportation available, I guess." I was playing it stupid. But I was staring at her breasts now.

"What about the car in the driveway?"

"My father's Mustang?"

"Yeah."

"He'd kill me."

"But you'd drive me home if I asked. You'd do it for me, right?"

My god, she had a look just then. And she leaned forward, put her hand on my leg and kissed me again, a softer kiss this time. And one that lasted a long time.

"Yes," I said, losing a battle in my head. I'd had one glass of wine. I didn't have a license. My father had let me drive the family car out in the country on some dirt roads a few times. But he'd never ever let me drive his old reconditioned Mustang.

"Yes," I said. "I'll drive you."

Chapter Eleven

I hadn't driven a car with that much power before. The Mustang was old but my father kept it in perfect condition. Dark metal-flake blue, eight cylinders, leather bucket seats. A muscle car, a mean machine, a true gas-guzzling destroyer of the environment.

The car was the one thing about my father that showed any sign of impracticality or recklessness. But when he drove the car, he babied it. As far as I knew, he never screeched the tires or drove over the speed limit.

Maybe he did that on the sly, when he was away from home and none of us could see him. But I doubted it.

Jeanette sank down in the seat and looked tired. Sleepy but sexy. I had to reach across her to put her seatbelt on when it looked like she wasn't going to do it for herself. My hand accidentally touched her breast, and she suddenly seemed more awake—she held it there for a second and then let go. Life was getting more interesting by the minute.

We were still parked in our driveway in front of my house. I was sure the nosy neighbors would be watching. "I've got to get you home," I said, sounding a little too much like my own father. A man doing the right thing.

I put on my own seatbelt, started the car and then slowly, oh so carefully, backed out of the driveway. Jeanette started to sing something I thought I'd heard on the radio. She was in a dreamy, faraway state. In some ways, I envied her. I wanted to be there with her—far away, light-headed, the two of us alone in a fantasy world.

But that wasn't going to happen. I had to stay focused. Ten blocks there, ten blocks back. Put the car in the exact spot. No one would ever suspect a thing. I was actually a little pleased with myself that things were going to be fine. I got that little buzz again. Here I was, breaking the rules, living a notch closer to the edge. What was that silly thing my grandfather used to say? "If you see an open door on an airplane, just jump out. You'll find a parachute on the way down." He was joking, but I understood now what he meant.

Jeanette kind of rolled her head side to side as she sang. Oh boy. I was hoping her parents weren't home.

When we passed the police car stopped by the side of the road, I kept my eyes straight ahead. I didn't notice if there was actually anyone in the car. But I knew better than to look suspicious. Drive sensibly, I kept telling myself. Stay cool. Be alert. Pretend you've been driving for years.

I would have done just that if Jeanette hadn't put her hand on my leg. That's when I ran straight through the stop sign.

I held my breath, realizing what I'd just done. Then I let out a big exhale when we were across the street. No cars had been coming. We were lucky. The parachute found me.

Or not.

It took a few minutes for the police car to catch up. I saw it approach in the rearview mirror, praying that the cop hadn't seen me roll through the stop sign. No such luck. The flashing red lights came on and my heart leaped into my throat. I gently took Jeanette's hand off my thigh and she giggled.

As I slowed and pulled over to the curb, I said, "Jeanette, I need you to act very, very cool right now."

"What?" She turned and saw the police car and the flashing lights. "Oh, crap," she said way too loud.

"Crap is right. Sit up and look normal."

"Oh my god. I think I'm going to have another panic attack."

"Just sit there. Don't say anything."

So now this once groggy girl was suddenly

looking wide awake and scared to death. "My parents are going to kill me," she said.

"Shh."

The man who got out of the police car was not wearing a uniform. That seemed a little odd. I rolled down the window and, without looking up at him, heard a voice say, "Step out of the car, please."

So I stepped out of the car. That's when I discovered it was the cop who had questioned me about the robbery, Detective Solway. I could tell he recognized me right away.

Before he said anything, he leaned past me and looked in at Jeanette. Jeanette was just staring straight ahead and breathing funny.

Detective Solway straightened back up and gave me a hard look. "Umm," he began, "I saw you run that stop sign...Sean, right?"

I nodded.

"Sean, they put those stop signs there for a reason."

"Yes, sir," I said. Part of me was really scared. Part of me wanted to run away from there, but another part of me found this scene both challenging and exhilarating.

"Did you do it on purpose or were you distracted?"

"Distracted."

He tilted toward the girl. "I can see why. She okay?"

"She's fine. I was just driving her home."

"Can I see your license?"

"Not really."

"Don't have one?"

"Nope."

"Your father's Mustang?"

"Yep."

"He's gonna be royally pissed."

"You better believe it."

Solway turned away for a minute and then turned back. "Sean, I'm not officially on duty right now. Just stopped by the house to pick up something. But when I saw you run through that stop sign, I figured I better try to serve and protect, you know what I'm saying?"

I nodded.

"I remember our little interview. I put the pieces of that Burger Heaven robbery together. Given what happened that night, I reckon you did the right thing. You held it together and you might have saved a couple of lives."

"What do you mean?"

"Last night there was another robbery at a convenience store in the north end of town. The woman there—an old woman who owned the place—refused to hand over the hard-earned cash, and she got shot. She's in the hospital but she'll recover. Description of the thugs sounds like they were the same ones who held you up."

I suddenly had a flashback to that night: the door opening, the gun, the adrenaline rush. Handing over the cash. And then looking into those eyes—the crazed eyes of the one pointing the gun straight at me with two hands. It was like a high-definition photograph. And then something clicked. I'd seen those eyes somewhere before.

I stood silently. My mind was somewhere else.

"Look," Solway said, "let's pretend this didn't happen. I like you. At least I think I do. And I've got enough on my plate right now. You have to promise me, though, to stop for every goddamn stop sign you ever see again in your life."

"I promise," I said.

"Then you drive this girl home and put your daddy's car back right over the oil stain in the driveway. And stay off the road until you have a license."

"Yes, sir."

"And if you have any other bit of information, any tiny sliver of a detail you forgot to tell me about that night at Burger Heaven, you call, okay? We don't have a lot to go on—nothing is matching up with past offenders."

"I'll do that."

"Good. Drive safe."

Chapter Twelve

Jeanette didn't speak to me the next day at school. I waved once when I saw her down the hallway, but if she saw me, she didn't wave back. When I had a chance to think about her—and I had lots of time for that during a totally boring math class—the rational part of my brain was telling me she was nothing but trouble and I should stay away. But the other part of my brain—the one that now ruled—was saying she was nothing but trouble and that was what I was so attracted to.

I tried to catch up with her after school, but just as I did, she was getting into a car. Her mother had come to pick her up. This probably meant she got some grief when she had arrived home the day before. Looked like I was on my own.

My father hadn't noticed that I had driven the Mustang. I had parked it in the same spot and returned his keys to the key rack. That part had been almost too easy.

I couldn't face the thought of just going home and watching TV or doing homework. Ever since the robbery, I'd been restless. I used to be happy to play video games or watch TV, but not anymore. I thought about my grandfather again and how much I missed him. I wondered if I was anything like he'd been when he was growing up.

I decided to head back downtown and see if I could find Priscilla.

I knocked on the door of the shelter and asked about her. "You a relative?" the woman who answered the door asked.

"No. A friend."

"Sorry, you can't come in."

"I know. I've been told that before. Is Priscilla here?"

"She was this morning but she's probably out on the street by now. Are you the one who brought her back yesterday?"

"Yes."

"Priscilla gets some rough treatment out there sometimes. People make fun of her. Say rude things."

"Can't anybody do anything about that?"

She shrugged. "Nah. No one pays attention to people like Priscilla."

"Does she find her way back each night?" I asked.

"Not all the time. Sometimes one of us goes looking, but we don't always find her."

"Where does she sleep?"

"Wherever she decides to lie down."

"I'll go take a look," I said. I was haunted by the image of an older woman like Priscilla just sleeping in a doorway or among the trash somewhere. I'd seen stories on TV about street people being beat up or even set on fire. I wondered if that could happen here. As I walked away, I looked around at the trash on the street, at the closed storefronts and the graffiti. And I thought, yeah, anything could happen here.

I walked three blocks east and then doubled back west on a parallel street. There I found Priscilla knocking on the door of a dilapidated brick house. A rather angry-looking bald man was opening the door as I approached.

"I'm home," I heard Priscilla say.

"You're not home," the man said. "This is my home, not yours. Now go away."

"But this is my home," she said in a shaky voice.

"Priscilla," I said as I walked toward her.

She turned but didn't recognize me at all. I saw the fear now in her face.

"It's me," I said. "Doyle."

"You're not Doyle," she snapped back.

"What the hell is this?" the man asked me. "Why is she here banging on my door?"

"It's okay. She's just confused," I told him.

"She's not confused," he said angrily. "She's crazy. This woman should be locked up." He turned and went back inside and slammed the door.

Priscilla put her face in her hands and began to sob. I touched her shoulder to try to walk her back down the steps, but she pulled away. "You're not Doyle," she repeated. "Doyle's dead."

"I know. I'm sorry. But we met before, remember?"

"No."

"The sandwich. The chips."

She looked up and I could see her face was wet with tears. It took a couple of seconds but then something clicked. "I do know you."

"Yes."

"You were that boy."

"Yes."

"The polite one."

"Right. My name's Sean."

"Sean."

I could see the homeowner's ugly face in the window now. He was waving at us to go away.

I gently guided Priscilla down the steps and back toward the street. "Here," she said, opening her purse. "I want you to have this." She handed me a toy truck. "I found it," she said. "Boys like to play with trucks."

"Thanks," I said. "I like it. Are you hungry?"

"I used to be."

"Would you like something to eat?"

"Pie. I would really like pie."

"Okay. Pie it is."

Back on Queen Street, I found a little restaurant called Phil's. But apparently Phil had also had some trouble with Priscilla before. "She's not allowed in here," Phil said. I knew his name because he wore a baseball cap that said *I'm Phil* on the front.

"Please, Phil," I said. "She just wants a piece of pie."

"The last time she came in, she peed on the seat." He said it as if Priscilla wasn't there at all, as if she didn't matter. A few customers turned and looked at us.

"If she causes any trouble, we'll leave right away, I promise."

"No," Phil said. "I've tried being nice to her before. It always comes back to bite me in the ass."

Priscilla looked hurt again. Rejected. Like a little girl who'd just been slapped. She was ready to cry again.

I could see Phil was damn serious. I held out a five-dollar bill. "Then it's pie to go, please," I said, although I wanted to tell Phil where to shove the pie.

Phil dropped his guard ever so slightly. "Apple or pumpkin?" he said. "That's all we got."

"Apple," Priscilla said. "Two pieces of apple pie, please."

Chapter Thirteen

Back on the street, I looked for a place to sit down with an old woman who wanted to eat apple pie. I carried the Styrofoam container in one hand and held on to Priscilla's arm with my other hand. It was a slow parade to the little triangle of a park on the corner. We found an empty park bench covered in graffiti and carvings. It wasn't much of a park—no grass, just packed dirt, no swing sets, no flowers. Trash scattered around all the weary-looking shrubs.

Priscilla was happy enough once I cracked the lid on the Styrofoam box and handed her the plastic fork. I thought about Priscilla and her life, and I wondered how she'd ended up like this. Maybe it was one of those things that could have happened to anyone. Maybe I'd end up on the street some day. Luck of the draw, I guess.

Priscilla ate slowly, almost daintily. Neither one of us spoke just then, and a strange calmness came over me. It was like time had stopped.

I didn't exactly know what had drawn me back here today. Boredom maybe. Curiosity about what my father calls "how the other half lives." Genuine concern for this old demented woman—a woman who I could be kind to, yet who I doubted I could save. And I realized that I was changing. Everything about this past week was different. And now I was different too.

"Looks like rain," Priscilla said at last.

And it did. It looked like it could rain. I nodded. She smiled.

Monroe and his friend named J.L. came our way. Monroe smiled. J.L. did not.

"Hi, Priscilla," Monroe said. "Looks like your boyfriend bought you your favorite dessert."

Priscilla laughed, smiled at him and then smiled at me. "Sean just got a new truck," she said. It was the first time she'd used my name.

"Really?" Monroe said, looking around the street. "Where's it parked, Sean?"

Priscilla giggled. "Show him."

I gingerly took the toy truck out of my jacket pocket and placed it on the palm of my hand.

Priscilla laughed out loud just then and so did Monroe. But not J.L. He had remained standing sideways to us, nervously looking down the street as if watching for something. But then he made a sudden turn and was looking right at me, a wary, agitated look in his eyes.

And then it hit me. I recognized those eyes.

As he turned quickly away, I pretended

that nothing had changed. The first drops of rain fell lightly on my forehead.

"See," Priscilla said, "I told you it would rain."

"Always does on a picnic," Monroe said. "It's either that or ants."

"Time to get you home," I told Priscilla.

"Guess you know the drill," Monroe said. "Don't get wet."

J.L. had already begun to walk away. He'd never said a single word. Monroe followed him.

We didn't move until the pie was all gone. I tossed the Styrofoam container in the nearly full wire garbage can and led Priscilla back to the shelter. I turned back a couple of times to see if anyone was following us. I was getting more nervous by the minute.

The raindrops were sporadic. My hair was wet, but Priscilla didn't seem to have a drop on her. She noticed me looking at her. "My mother taught me how to walk between the raindrops," she explained. "It takes practice but it can be done. I taught Doyle to do it when he was young."

The woman at the shelter was happy to see Priscilla returning. I didn't hang around for any polite conversation. I wanted to make sure that Priscilla was safely inside, and when I was back on the now-empty street in the drizzling rain, I began to run. Three blocks away I caught the bus headed back to my neighborhood. I sat alone in my seat, staring out the window as the rain increased. I considered my options. And none of them looked good.

When I got home, I phoned Jeanette. I didn't know who else to call.

"Why are you calling me?" she asked, sounding annoyed.

"I have to talk to you about something."

"My parents knew I was drinking. I threw up in the bathroom. Why did you let me drink so much?"

"It wasn't my idea."

"I thought you were so dependable."

It was a no-win situation, but right then I had something else on my mind. "Jeanette, I saw the guy today."

"What guy?"

"The guy who held the gun on me that night."

"What do you mean, you saw him? They had ski masks on."

"Yeah, but I saw his eyes. I'm almost positive that I know who he is."

"I don't think so. None of us could have identified either one of those guys who came in."

"You were in the back. I was in the front. I looked him straight in the eyes. You heard Solway. They think the same guy shot someone in a store. What should I do?"

"Nothing," she said without losing a beat.

"Nothing?"

"If you identify him, you could get hurt," she said.

"Don't they have some kind of room you sit in where you can see out but they can't see in?" I asked.

"I guess so, but did you meet this person face-to-face already?"

"Yes," I said.

"Then if he gets arrested, he's gonna want to figure out who snitched."

"Snitched isn't exactly the word."

"Sean, don't be stupid," she said. "Do nothing. Don't get involved."

And she hung up the phone. I held it for a long time as if waiting for more, but the dial tone came on. And I knew then she was right. What was I thinking? Two things were clear. I could not go back downtown again. And I would not say a word.

Chapter Fourteen

I never knew my grandparents on my mother's side. They lived in England and had visited only three times when I was a kid. They were polite and kind, I suppose, just not all that interested in me. He was an investment banker involved in the flow of international money, and she was a woman who spent her time with other women married to investment bankers. I think they gave my parents money for me to go to college. If I decided to go.

On my father's side, my grandmother died when I was very young, but my wonderful crazy grandfather, Hank, hung on until that fateful ultralight accident. What I remember most about him was his energy, his high spirits and his unlimited optimism. Whenever anything went wrong, he'd always say, "It will all work out in the end" or "We're going to turn this around into something positive."

My father had decided not to follow in his father's footsteps and was now a guy who believed in safety and caution. Two of his favorite words. And my mother, I believe, admired him for those assets. She claimed that she had lived a few reckless years in her early twenties before marrying, but she would never talk about it. Both of my parents had done an excellent job of keeping me safe for over sixteen years.

"We think you should find another job," my father said at the dinner table that night. "Or concentrate on your studies, maybe. Prepare yourself academically for university."

"I'm going back to my job," I told him. "I know it doesn't seem like much of a job, but I like it." I wondered which, if any, of my former coworkers would be back there when I showed up Saturday night.

"Then we'll get Ernesto to switch your times."

"I like working nights," I insisted.

"But we're worried about you," my mother chimed in.

"I know. But I'll be all right. I need to do this for me."

I had a list of things I wanted to change about me. I wanted to be more assertive. I wanted to be more adventurous. I wanted to be more willing to take chances and I wanted to be able to make my own decisions. Including the one about going to the cops about what I thought I knew about the gunman.

I guess I wanted to be more like my grandfather. I had thought about this more than once as I got older. What would old Hank do in this situation? Once, in an unguarded moment, when Hank had been drinking, I think, he took me aside and whispered,

"Sean, you have to really live your life. You have to experience everything you can." I didn't really get it. But it was the way he said it.

It was odd to think that Jeanette was claiming to be the voice of reason. Here was a screwed-up girl who couldn't get her own life straight, and she was telling me to keep my mouth shut about a criminal. But she was right. If I opened my mouth and went to the cops, somebody back there on the street would be waiting to get me. I would be in over my head. There would be a gun involved or a knife or god knows what. It could be violent. The cops wouldn't be able to protect me.

The next day I went to school and failed a history test I had not studied for. I was a useless lab partner in biology and discovered that trying to read a nineteenth-century English novel was not all it was cracked up to be. Jeanette avoided me as best she could. Whatever spark there was between us before was gone. I still thought she was really hot, but I knew that nothing was going to happen between us.

I began thinking about other girls I knew and plotting a way to actually get noticed by them. I had always been kind of invisible but I needed to work on getting noticed. I was looking forward to returning to work on Saturday. You never knew who might walk in through those glass doors.

But right then I felt like I was going nowhere. The only woman in my life was Priscilla, and I was not at all sure it was a good idea for me to trek downtown to see her again. After school, I holed up in my room and played a couple of video games I'd been ignoring. They weren't nearly as much fun now as I remembered them to be. I got bored and fell asleep early.

My father was surprised to see me in the kitchen while he was eating breakfast the next morning. "You're up early," he said, setting down the morning newspaper.

"I was hungry," I said and popped a couple of pieces of bread in the toaster.

That's when I saw it. The story on the front page of the paper.

There'd been another robbery. At a gas station this time. And someone had been shot and killed.

My father watched me as I read the story. The blood drained from my face. There was a picture of the victim, a university student who had been working part-time at night at the service station. And there was a fuzzy in-store security cam image of the guy holding the gun. You couldn't see his face but it was a guy with a ski mask. I was pretty sure it was J.L. I even recognized the sweatshirt he was wearing.

I prayed that I was wrong, but I knew I had to go talk to Detective Solway, and I didn't want to give my father or anyone a chance to talk me out of it. Once I made that first step into the police station, I knew my life might never be the same again.

But it was a step I had to take.

Chapter Fifteen

I knew that my father was looking at me and I tried to act natural. And then I realized something was different. My father was not dressed for work. No suit and no tie. I looked at the clock. It was 8:30.

"Aren't you going to be late for work?" I asked.

"I got fired," he said.

"What? Not again!"

"Fired. Done. Finished." He tried to smile. "You could say I'm on vacation."

This didn't make any sense. "There must have been some mistake, right?"

"No, I guess you wouldn't call it a mistake. I wasn't willing to go along with what my boss wanted. So they fired me."

"What did they want you to do?"

"It's probably not a big deal. In fact, it's probably done all the time. You know all those twenty-five-cent slot machines in the casino?"

"Sure."

"You can set the odds of winning on them. It's supposedly regulated by the government, but everyone is pretty sloppy about it."

"But you don't work on the slot machines. You're an accountant."

"Right. But somebody along the way reset the odds of winning on those machines. They did it months ago. And as a result, my company was making higher profits. Significantly higher profits. The odds of a customer winning went down. The odds of us making more money went up. I was just curious about why our revenues were so much higher on those machines."

"And?"

"And they told me to look the other way."

"Why didn't you?"

"I'm not sure. I guess I didn't think they'd fire me. I just thought I was doing my job by keeping them on track."

"But they didn't see it that way."

"I went out on a limb. I said we should come clean and admit the mistake, make an apology, pay a fine or whatever and move on."

"Only it wasn't a mistake," I said.

"Right."

"Can't you fight this?" I asked.

"I probably could but I'm not sure I will. I just know I did the right thing."

"Balls to the wall," I said, not exactly sure why.

"What?"

"It's what Hank used to say, remember?" I said.

My father suddenly smiled. "Balls to the wall. I do remember that."

"So this is your ultralight," I said, wondering if he'd understand.

He smiled again but said nothing.

I looked down at the newspaper and took a deep breath.

"Dad, I guess I have to tell you something."

He saw the look on my face. "About the car?" he asked. "Don't worry about that. I keep an eye on the odometer and noticed that it had a higher number on it than where I left it. Don't know why I do that. I just have a kind of photographic thing about numbers. Guess that's why I became an accountant. I was a little disappointed in you at first, but then I talked to your mother. She said she was surprised it took you this long, that it was quite a temptation."

"You're okay with that?" I asked.

"Now I am. This weekend, let's do it right. We'll go out to the country and you can drive all you want."

"I don't have a license. You know that."

"Balls to the wall," he said. "Want some more toast?"

"Sure."

As I stared down at the newspaper again, I suddenly realized I didn't know my father, not really. I'd always thought of him as the opposite of Hank, my grandfather. Now this.

As he popped the bread into the toaster and poured himself another cup of coffee, I stared at the photo of the victim in the paper again, a guy not much older than me. And I now understood that I wasn't in this alone after all.

"I think I know who held the gun that night. I think I can identify him."

My father had his back to me and he seemed to freeze. Then he turned around slowly.

"I could be wrong," I said, "but I don't think so. I met a guy on the street. I've seen him twice in fact. I was already pretty sure it was him but I didn't want to get involved. But now this." I pushed the newspaper toward him. He looked down at it and saw the photo of the victim.

"What are you going to do?" he asked.

"I don't think I have a choice," I said.

"You always have a choice. You could do nothing. The police are going to get serious now that someone's been killed. This guy can't keep getting away with this."

"Detective Solway told me they don't have much to go on."

"That may have changed. Now they have this picture from the security cam."

I looked at the fuzzy image again. "It's not much to go on."

"No, it isn't," he admitted.

"Will you drive me down to the police station?"

The toast popped up just then. My father looked frightened.

"Part of me wants to talk you out of this," he said.

"I know. I thought about what it might mean," I said. "It could be a rough ride."

"I don't want anything bad to happen to you."

"I know that too," I said. "But if I go down there now, this guy with the gun could be off the street today. I'm fairly sure of that. If I let it go until tomorrow or the next day or wait for the cops to figure it out on their own..."

I didn't finish the sentence. I just let it hang there.

Chapter Sixteen

My father called Detective Solway and told him we were coming. He drove me to the police station in the Mustang. It somehow felt right.

Solway asked him to sit in a waiting room and led me into the same room where he had questioned me before. I could tell he was upset about something.

I told Solway what I thought. He was skeptical. "He had a ski mask on and you only saw his eyes?"

"Yes."

"But you believe you've met him on the street, and you can describe what he looks like?"

"His name is J.L. I don't know what it stands for and I don't know his last name, but it shouldn't be that hard to find out."

"Why didn't you come in before?"

"I don't know."

"Where did you see him?"

"Downtown. South Main."

"You might have saved a life if you'd come to us sooner," he said after a long pause. "You know how hard it is these days to get anyone to come forward? Young men in gangs get knifed or beat up and they refuse to say a word about who did it. Even little kids don't want to point the finger at the bully. No one wants to be the snitch." He rubbed his forehead and looked at me. "But you're different, right?"

He was silent for a minute. "Look, it's just that sometimes someone starts out offering information and then they crap out on me. They don't follow through. This happens. A lot. Are you going to be able to follow through?"

"Yeah," I said, "I'll follow through." I remembered that moment again, staring at the gun, looking in those insane eyes.

"If your guy is smart, he's long gone from here by now. He's done too much damage. But my guess is he isn't smart. Just lucky. But I think his luck just ran out. I'm going to get Jack Kacer in here and you're going to give him features to work with."

Solway went away. He came back with a heavyset guy who looked like the weight of the world was on his shoulders. He sat down at a computer in the corner and nodded.

"Eyes first, right?"

We went through forty images of just eyes until I saw them.

"Those are his," I said.

"Not his really. They're computer generated. But it's a start. Now we have to come up with a face. You say you saw this guy without the mask?"

"Yeah."

Solway said, "I'm going to run 'J.L.' through the system and see if anything comes up." He left the room.

Jack put me through a series of head shapes, chins, noses. It was slow and tedious and eventually we came up with a face that was not quite right. Over an hour had passed.

"Can I take a break?" I asked.

"Sure," he said.

I went out of the room. My father was still in the waiting room, looking nervous. "Everything okay?" he asked.

"I think so. But I'm having second thoughts."

"Me too," my father said, and he gave me a hug. He hadn't done that in a long time.

Solway came our way just then. He had a handful of manila files with him. He pretended he didn't see us. "No J.L. came up, but I've got a dozen or so here with first-name and middle-name initials that match that. Ready to look at them?"

We went back into the room and Jack Kacer showed me a newly revised face. "What about this one?" he asked.

"Closer," I said.

"Good," Solway said. "At least now we have some pieces. Look at these."

The eighth file was that of someone named James Leroy Pender. It wasn't a recent photo, but I was pretty sure it was him. I looked up at the computer likeness, then at the real photo.

Kacer did a quick scan of the file photo with a wireless hand scanner and pulled it up on his screen almost instantly. "Now we're cooking," he said. "What do we need to do to it?"

I didn't realize at first what he was asking me. "Um...make his face a little thinner. The eyes a little crazier. Shorter hair." Kacer was clicking away with the mouse. "Now give him three or four days of not shaving."

It was him. It was J.L.

"We still don't know if he's our target," Solway told Kacer. "But this is the guy Sean thinks is the one. We haven't seen him in a while. All I have here is petty theft, selling marijuana and a break-and-enter. But it could be he got himself in deeper with the drugs. That's what sometimes makes them more reckless. Some of them get hooked on the risk in a holdup. We'll bring in this James Leroy Pender and see what he has to say."

Jack Kacer looked even more tired than before. “Good work, kid,” he said to me.

Solway’s look didn’t say anything of the sort. He turned to me. “All this is based on what you say, Sean. You know that, right? Things have just gotten a bit more serious. What are the odds that this J.L. person will know it was you who made the connection?”

“I don’t really know but I think the odds are pretty good.”

“If we get anything at all to work with, we can detain him. If not, he may be back on the street in no time. I’d steer clear of him if I were you. And even if we keep him, he may have friends.”

I was thinking of Keeg, Vicente and Robert. Maybe even Monroe. Was it possible they were in on these robberies too? “What do I do?”

“Go home. Go to school. Avoid being alone anywhere. And avoid going anywhere near South Main for a long, long while.”

Chapter Seventeen

Later that day I got a call from Solway. My father and I picked up the phone at the same time, and I know he stayed on the line.

"We found J.L. and we found a gun—looks like it's the gun he used to kill the kid working at the gas station," Solway said. "This means that you will be a whole lot less important in his conviction. It means the whole case doesn't hang on just you. You see what I'm saying?"

"So that's it? I don't have to go into a room and identify him or anything like that?" I asked.

There was a pause. "No. Not yet anyway. We've got enough here to charge him and keep him in custody. But if this goes to trial, you may have to appear as a witness, and yes, J.L. would be in the courtroom. As long as we know how to find you, you don't need to do anything more for now."

"I'm not going anywhere," I said, but I was wondering what it would feel like to stand up in that courtroom.

"Maybe he'll plead guilty. He hasn't told us who his accomplice was yet, so we still have some legwork to do."

"Right."

"Thanks for sticking your neck out," said Solway. "It's rare for people to come forward."

As I hung up, I felt a swirling mix of emotions. Relief, I suppose. Satisfaction in doing the right thing. Anxiety about what I might have to do further down the line. And then a sense of confusion—loss even. I had put myself right in the middle of this thing and, for now, it was over. I would get back to my own life. Suddenly that didn't look at all interesting.

A lot had changed in a very short amount of time. I couldn't go back to being the person I had been before. But I wasn't sure I knew exactly who I was anymore. I pictured myself walking straight across that highway. I saw myself in the middle of wet, sloppy kisses with Jeanette. And I could see myself walking around those dirty city streets with Priscilla. I felt like I'd made a commitment to her as a friend. I couldn't just abandon her.

I decided not to tell anyone about my part in identifying J.L. No one knew but my parents and the police. Maybe it would stay that way.

My father knocked on my door.

"Come in," I called.

He didn't say anything at first, just smiled and gave me a hug. "Hank would have been proud of you," he said. "I know I am."

My father persuaded my mother that it was okay for me to go back to work. So after dinner on Saturday, I put on my cheesy blue and white uniform, and my father drove me to work. "Good luck," he said.

Inside Burger Heaven, everything looked the same. Ernesto was trying to look cheerful. "You wanna work the grill tonight?"

He knew I hated cooking burgers. "I'd rather go back on cash."

"You're okay with that?"

"Sure. It has a much higher entertainment value," I said.

I'm not sure he got the joke, but he said, "Whatever. Sure. Cash it is."

I was shocked to see Cam. Ernesto asked him if he wanted to work the grill. He surprised me by saying he wanted to be up front too. When the phone rang, I was left standing face-to-face with Cam.

"Sorry, dude," he said, looking down at the floor. "Sorry about the stuff I said. I thought about what you did. It took a while. But it sank in. I got it. After I saw the thing on the news about the gas station. Oh, man. It could have been me."

"It could have been both of us," I said.

"Next guy with a gun that comes in through that door, I'm letting you call it."

"Thanks," I said. "I'm kind of hoping there is no next guy with a gun."

"Lot of freaking crazies out there, Sean."

"I've noticed," I said. I looked up at the ceiling then. "Check it out," I said.

Cam looked up. Ernesto had installed new security cameras. There was a big sign on the wall behind the counter too: *Smile. You are being videotaped.*

"Anything happens now," I said, "we can watch the replay on the six o'clock news."

Cam shook his head. "Don't know if that will stop the crazies, man."

"Maybe not."

"Did you hear they caught one of the guys?" he said. "The one with the gun?"

"Yeah, I read that," I said.

"Lacey's not coming back and neither is Riley. I don't think Jeanette's parents will let her come back. Didn't I see you hanging out with her at school?"

I had been thinking about Jeanette, wanting to call her and ask her out again. "We had a little thing," I said. "But it's over."

"Too bad," he said. "She's hot."

I shrugged. "Why did you come back?"

He looked puzzled. "I'm not sure. I didn't think I would. I felt I had to do it, I guess."

I understood, though. Something to do with facing your own fears, your own nightmares. Sure, this was just a crummy job selling burgers for minimum pay. We weren't going to do it for the rest of our lives, but we weren't going to let the "crazies" make us huddle at home in fear. I didn't say any of this to Cam, but I think it was what we were both feeling, and I was totally freaked to suddenly realize how much he and I were alike.

I had already assumed that Jeanette would not be back. Miss Anxiety Attack. No way she'd put herself in such a stressful situation.

But I was looking up at the video monitor on the wall when she walked in. Even on the TV screen she looked nervous, but she looked so sweet in the Burger Heaven uniform.

I watched as Ernesto walked from behind the counter and greeted her.

She didn't say anything at all to me, but she smiled. She didn't even look at Cam.

"Look who gets to cook hamburgers," Cam said. But she gave no reply.

A couple of other workers showed up to join us—all older. One, with a name tag that said *Dave*, who looked like somebody's grandfather, and one named Tony, who looked like a bouncer from a bar. They'd obviously worked there before but on different shifts.

There was some confusion and tension as the earlier shift turned things over to us. Pretty soon three really rowdy teenagers came in, and things seemed a little tense. Then they ordered— so politely that Cam and I looked at each other, amazed. Ernesto stayed around, something he'd never done before when I was working there.

And it turned out to be a perfectly normal evening. When my break came around, I sat with Jeanette at a table near the window. At first she just sat there, looking at her reflection in the glass.

"I forgot just how much this job sucks," she said.

"Then why did you come back?"

"Because I knew you'd be here. And I wanted to prove something to you. That I'm not a complete flake."

I was going to say something about her not being a flake. Instead I smiled at her, picked up one of her French fries and said, "Cooking greasy hamburgers over a hot grill proves you're not a flake?"

She smiled back now. "Yes. It does." She grabbed the French fry from me playfully and put it in her mouth.

I decided that we'd never really given ourselves a chance to get to know each other. And now we would. Very slowly. And it would be very different than before.

Lesley Choyce is a prolific author, a publisher and a lifelong surfer. He lives in Nova Scotia.